Volcanoes

Ted O'Hare

Bethany, Missouri

Photo Credits:
Cover © USGS; Title Page © Craig Hansen; Page 5 © Marco Regalia; Page 7 © Armentrout; Page 9 ©
Bychkov Kirill Alexandrovi; Page 11 © Bryan Buscovicki, Vera Bogaerts; Page 13 © USGS/ Mike Doukas; Page 15
© Lanica Klein; Page 16 © Helen Shorey; Page 17 © NASA; Page 18 © Todd Hackwelder; Page 19 © USGS;
Page 21 © Paul Hart; Page 22 © USGS/ Mike Lisowski

Cataloging-in-Publication Data

O'Hare, Ted, 1961-
     Volcanoes / Ted O'Hare. — 1st ed.
     p. cm. — (Natural disasters)

     Includes bibliographical references and index.
     Summary: Illustrations and text introduce what volcanoes are,
what they do and some specific volcanoes in history.
     ISBN-13: 978-1-4242-1404-4 (lib. bdg. : alk. paper)
     ISBN-10: 1-4242-1404-1 (lib. bdg. : alk. paper)
     ISBN-13: 978-1-4242-1494-5 (pbk. : alk. paper)
     ISBN-10: 1-4242-1494-7 (pbk. : alk. paper)

     1. Volcanoes—Juvenile literature. [1. Volcanoes.
2. Natural disasters.] I. O'Hare, Ted, 1961- II. Title.
III. Series.
     QE521.3.O43 2007
     551.21—dc22

First edition
© 2007 Fitzgerald Books
802 N. 41st Street, P.O. Box 505
Bethany, MO 64424, U.S.A.
Printed in China
Library of Congress Control Number: 2006911287

Table of Contents

What Is a Volcano?

A volcano is like a mountain with a hole in the middle of its top. This opening allows hot matter from inside the Earth's **crust** to escape into the air.

When a volcano spews forth its contents, it is said to **erupt**. Gases and matter may come pouring out of the volcano.

5

The outer layer of the Earth is made up of slabs of rock. These are known as **tectonic plates**. The plates rest on the interior, known as the **mantle**. The very center of the Earth is called the **core**.

Inside Earth

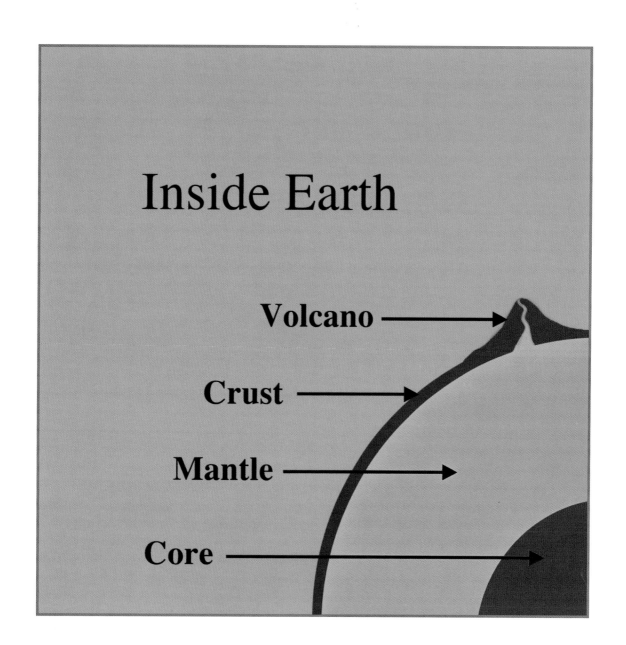

Volcano ⟶

Crust ⟶

Mantle ⟶

Core ⟶

Much of the rock in the Earth's mantle is very hot, sometimes as high as 2,700° F (1,480° C). The core is hotter still.

Magma inside a volcano is affected by pressure. The pressure forces magma out of the volcano in the form of lava. The lava contains gas, smoke, ash, and pieces of rock.

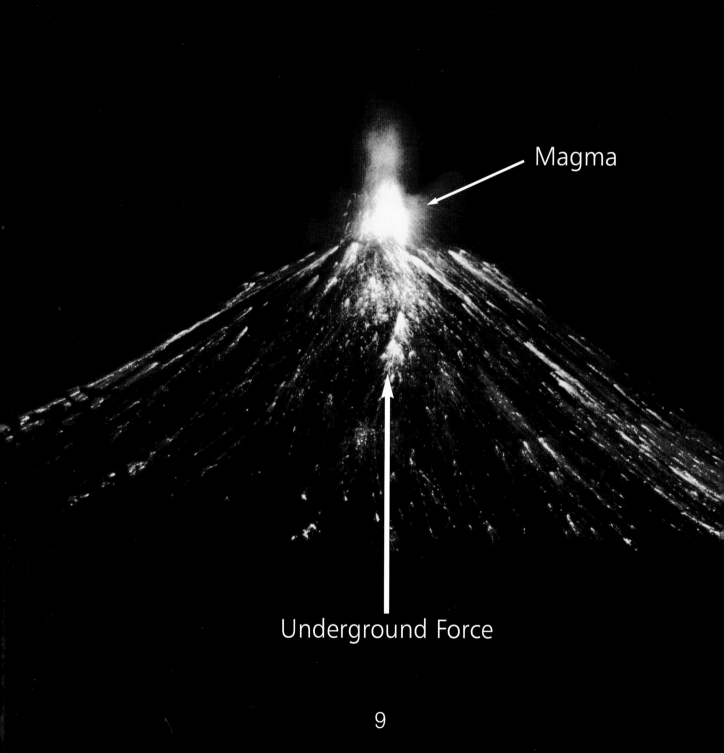

Magma

Underground Force

There are about 500 **active** volcanoes around the world. Many of them are located near the edges of continents.

More than half of them are on land surrounding the Pacific Ocean. This area is known as the "Ring of Fire."

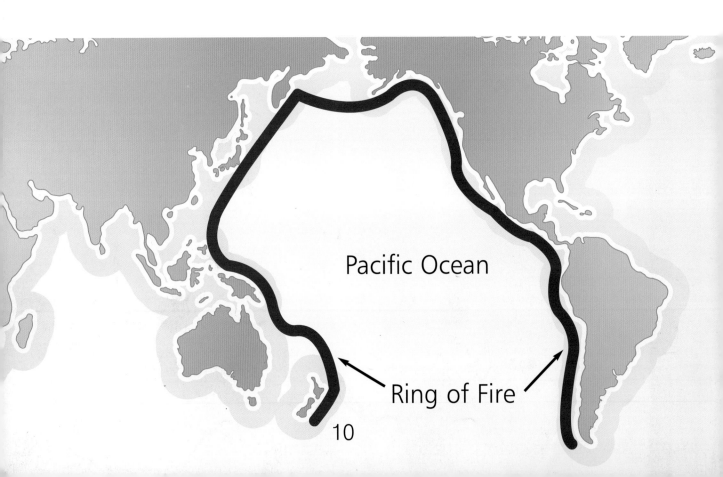

Pacific Ocean

Ring of Fire

Magma

Mount St. Helens

Many volcanoes lie **dormant** for years and years until they erupt. Such a volcano is Mount St. Helens in Washington State. Mount St. Helens erupted with terrific force in 1980.

Rock and mud flowed everywhere. Hot ash buried rivers and roads. The lava also destroyed many plants and animals, and 57 people died.

13

Mount St. Helens' explosion could be heard for many miles. Even today, the volcano simmers and smokes, although there have not been any major eruptions since.

Other Famous Volcanoes

A very long time ago, Mount Vesuvius, near Naples, Italy, suddenly exploded and killed thousands. The ash buried the famous city of Pompeii.

In 1883, a volcano named Krakatoa exploded with great force, killing around 36,000 people. The sound could be heard more than 2,000 miles (3,218 kilometers) away.

Much of the Hawaiian Islands are made up of volcanoes. The world's largest volcano is Mauna Loa, most of which lies beneath the sea's surface.

Ash

Mount Pinatubo, in the Philippines, erupted in 1991 after 500 years of lying dormant.

Dangerous Volcanoes

Volcanic eruptions can damage nearby land. People who live close to a volcano will be in terrible danger if it erupts.

Studying Volcanoes

   Scientists who study volcanoes are **volcanologists**. Sometimes they discover earth that has moved. They know that sometimes eruptions enrich soil and help new plants grow.

Glossary

active (AK tiv) — alive, possibly moving

core (KORR) — the Earth's hot center

crust (KRUST) — the Earth's hard outer layer

dormant (DOOR munt) — not active, but alive

erupt (ee RUPT) — to spew forth volcanic matter

magma (MAG muh) — melted rock under the Earth's surface

mantle (MANT ul) — the layer of earth between the crust and the core

tectonic plates (tek TAWN ik PLAYTZ) — pieces of the Earth's crust

volcanologists (VUL kun ahl uh jistz) — scientists who study volcanoes

Index

FURTHER READING

DK Publishing. *Volcanoes and Earthquakes (Eyewitness)*. DK Children's Books, 2004.
Editors, Time for Kids. *Time for Kids: Volcanoes*. HarperCollins, 2006.
Simon, Seymour. *Volcanoes*. HarperCollins, 2006.

WEBSITES TO VISIT

Because Internet links change so often, Fitzgerald Books has developed an online list of websites related to the subject of this book. This site is updated regularly. Please use this link to access the list: www.fitzgeraldbookslinks.com/nd/vol

ABOUT THE AUTHOR

Ted O'Hare is an author and editor of children's nonfiction books. Ted has written over fifty children's books over the past decade. Ted has worked for many publishing houses including the Macmillan Children's Book Group.